A TURKISH AFTERNOON

Olivia Bennett   Photographs by Christopher Cormack

Hamish Hamilton
London

GW00381507

'Come on, you two! It's time to go to the library.'
Yiğit and Mert are playing football in the garden. It is
nearly the end of the summer holidays. As a treat, Mum is
taking them and their little sister Yelda to a 'Turkish
Afternoon' at a local library.

2

Yiğit and Mert share a bedroom. It has pictures of Spiderman and the Incredible Hulk stuck on the walls. Yiğit drew them himself.

'Don't forget your tracksuit, Yiğit. After we have been to the library, we are going to see Dad at the factory. Then he is taking you with him to football practice.'

When they arrive at the library, Yiğit stops to read the poster in the window.
'Everyone is welcome to the Turkish Afternoon. Learn to dance and sing in Turkish.'

Yiğit's family are Turkish Cypriots. His grandparents left Cyprus and came to live in England 22 years ago. His mum was ten years old then. That is two years older than Yiğit is now. 'It must have been strange for Mum,' thinks Yiğit, 'I can't imagine moving to another country.'

'Come on, Yiğit. Stop daydreaming!' calls Mum. She can hear the Turkish music coming from the garden behind the library. They go into the garden and sit down to watch the dancers.

'I like the colours of their clothes,' says Mert.
'These dancers come from south-east Turkey. Most towns and villages have their own special costume,' explains Mum.

'Each dance tells a story. It might be the story of how they plant and harvest the fields around their village. Other dances are about their feelings and tell tales of sadness or anger or happiness – or perhaps a love story.'

'What about the instruments they are playing?'
'The pipe is called a zurna and the round drum is called a davul. These instruments are played at most village weddings and festivals.'

After the dancing is over, Yiğit and Mert look at the
bookstall. Some of the books are written in English and
others are in Turkish.
'This book is about a white mouse,' Yiğit tells his brother.
Yiğit is learning to read in English and Turkish. 'You can
take all these books out of the library. They have tapes of
Turkish music which you can borrow, too.'

'Let's go and get some sweets,' says Mert. He can't read yet.
Roger works in the library. He is giving all the children
Turkish sweets and orange juice. Yiğit sees an open box of
Turkish delight. The Turkish name for this is lokum.

'Um! Delicious,' says
Yiğit. 'Lokums are my
favourite.'

9

Before they leave
the library, Yelda,
Mert and Yiğit
look at the posters
of Turkey.

'Anneanne and Dede went there on
holiday, didn't they?' asks Mert. He
calls his grandparents by Turkish
names for grandmother and
grandfather.
'Yes, and they took me back to
Cyprus when I was eight months old,'
replies Yiğit.
'I don't remember it, though!'

Dad's factory is quite near the library. On the way there, Mum buys a huge watermelon, called karpuz in Turkish. It has green stripes on the outside and is bright red inside. All the melons in the shop come from Cyprus.

'We need some bread and coffee, too, don't we, Mum?'
They buy some Turkish bread called çörek. It has sesame
seeds on the top.
'It's still warm from the oven,' says Yiğit. 'Can we buy some
olives too? I like the black ones best.'

'I like these green ones,' says Mum. 'They come from Cyprus.' The shop owner mixes them with chopped garlic, pieces of lemon and the seeds of a herb called coriander. 'Your grandmother is coming over for coffee tonight. I'll get these for her. We always had lots of olives at home.'

When they reach the factory, Yiğit runs to find his father.
'Dad, guess what? We've been watching Turkish dancing
and eating lokums.'
Yiğit's Dad has started his own business with a partner.
They have a small factory where they make suits, jackets
and coats. All the people who work in the factory, except
one, are Turkish Cypriots.

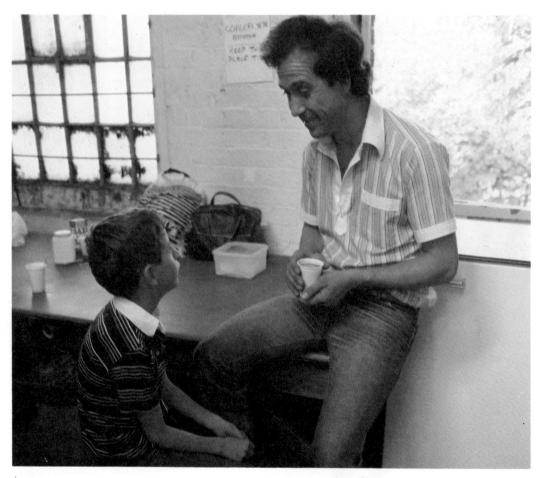

'Merhaba, Yiğit,' they call. Merhaba means hello. Everyone in the factory talks Turkish to each other. The sign by Yiğit's Dad says 'Keep this place tidy' in English and Turkish.

The factory is quite noisy. The sewing machines rattle away all day and Turkish music plays through a loudspeaker.

The factory is closing for the day. Everyone is going home.
Yiğit's Dad has a last word with the man who cuts the
patterns out of the rolls of cloth. First he draws the pattern
on some special paper. Then he lays the paper on top of the
material. This special paper is very thin and slightly sticky.
The cutter runs a warm iron over the paper pattern so that it
sticks to the cloth. This means it doesn't slip when he cuts
the shape out of the material.

This man is pressing a jacket which is nearly finished. He has a special iron. It sprays hot steam onto the jacket. Then he presses the lapels of the jacket with the iron so that they lie flat.

Yelda, Yiğit and Mert are tired of waiting for Dad.
'Let's play on the rolls of cloth!'
Dad sees them and tells them to go and play quietly in his office.
'You'll get too dirty rolling around on the floor like that.'

'Look,' says Yiğit, 'I'm drawing a spaceship.'
Mert watches him.

At last Dad has finished his work. He locks up the factory.
He and Yiğit go off to Clissold Park for their football practice.

19

Dad plays for a Turkish Cypriot team. They practise in the park every Thursday. On Sundays they play a match against another Turkish football team. He helps Yiğit tie his training shoes.

'I'd like to be a professional footballer when I grow up, Dad.'
'Then you'll have to train very hard. Let's start with those exercises I taught you. Follow what I do exactly. That's it. Touch your left toes with your right hand and your right toes with your left hand.'

Dad's team mates start to arrive. They let Yiğit join in their practice.

By 8 o'clock Yiğit is feeling a bit tired and very hungry. Dad takes him home for supper. Mum has cooked a hot meal of meat, beans, noodles, and some crushed wheat which is called bulgur. Yelda tries to take a mouthful of Yiğit's supper but he sees her!

'Ooh. Mum's cutting up the watermelon. Can I have some?'
'Bekle,' says Mum. It means 'wait' in Turkish. 'Finish your meat first and then you can have a slice.'
'I love karpuz,' says Mert, 'but I don't like the pips.'

'Anneanne and Dede are here,' calls Yiğit.
He has seen his grandparents arrive. They always speak in Turkish to their grandchildren and the children reply in Turkish.
'Mum is making coffee.'

She puts some water in the pot. It is called a cezve. Then she measures in one spoonful of coffee for each cup and adds some sugar. She stirs it carefully and lets the coffee slowly come to the boil. The coffee is very thick and strong.

'We went to a "Turkish Afternoon" at the library, Anneanne. Look at this book we borrowed. It's all in Turkish and there are lots of stories and pictures.'
'I'll come up soon and read it to you, Yiğit. I think it is time you had a bath and went to bed. It has been a long day, hasn't it?'

First published in Great Britain 1983 by
Hamish Hamilton Children's Books
Garden House, 57–59 Long Acre, London WC2E 9JZ
Copyright © 1983 by Hamish Hamilton
Photographs © 1983 by Hamish Hamilton
All rights reserved

British Library Cataloguing in Publication Data
Bennett, Olivia
A Turkish afternoon
1. Turkish Cypriots—Great Britain—Social Life
and customs—Juvenile literature
I. Title
941.0049435   DA125.T/
ISBN 0 241 11033 5

Printed in Spain